UNSUITABLE
FOR ADULTS

For MIKE, with thanks

UNSUITABLE
FOR ADULTS

TERRY JOHNSON

ff

faber and faber

LONDON · BOSTON

in association with the
Bush Theatre

First published in 1985
by Faber and Faber Limited
3 Queen Square London WC1N 3AU

Photoset by Wilmaset Birkenhead Wirral
Printed in Great Britain by
Whitstable Litho Whitstable Kent

British Library Cataloguing in Publication Data

Johnson, Terry
Unsuitable for adults.
I. Title
822'.94   PR6060.037/

ISBN 0-571-13773-3

Library of Congress Cataloging-in-Publication Data

Johnson, Terry, 1955–
Unsuitable for adults.
I. Title
PR6060.038U67   1986   822'.914   85-15959

ISBN 0-571-13773-3 (pbk.)

Unsuitable for Adults was first performed at the Bush Theatre, London, in January 1984. The cast was as follows:

KATE	Felicity Montagu
HARRY	Ivor Roberts
TISH	Joanne Pearce
NICK	Tim McInnerny
KEITH	Saul Jephcott
MAN	Roger Milner

Directed by	Mike Bradwell
Décor	Geoff Rose
Lighting	Alan O'Toole
Sound	Annie Hutchinson

CHARACTERS

KATE	Mid-twenties, dark, not pretty. Her clothes and manner a little self-consciously unfeminine. Comedian.
TISH	Mid-twenties, blonde, very pretty, high strung. Dressed attractively. A stripper.
NICK	Late twenties, tall, laconic, good-looking. A talented impersonator.
KEITH	Late twenties, homely. An untalented magician.
HARRY	Fifties, a northerner. A brewery publican.
MAN	Fifties, tall, gaunt.

SETTING

The upstairs room of a pub in Soho. The room is tall, early Georgian and once quite splendid with painted panels and cornice-work. Now, however, it is in a bad state. It has been decorated three times too often and the huge windows have been tackily blacked out with plywood. Remnants of last year's Christmas decorations are still hanging; a space for a dartboard which has now moved downstairs; redundant posters and notices . . . In one corner a small stage has been built. It is badly lit by a number of small coloured spotlights.

At the end of the play, the scene moves to a lonely stone cottage on Dartmoor. This can either be suggested in the midst of the main setting, or the setting moved out. The latter, of course, is preferable.

ACT ONE

*The lights are focused on the little stage. Littered around an empty
wooden stool is a girl's school uniform: blazer, blouse, tie, shoes,
socks and knickers. A cheap stereo tape deck is visible and plays
tacky music suitable for stripping to. A single figure sits looking at the
stage, hands deep in the pockets of a combat jacket. The lights
change, not very artistically. Enter* HARRY, *collecting glasses.*

HARRY: Time, gentlemen please! It's gone three o'clock now.
(KATE *turns round to look at him. She wears nothing feminine
and her hair is cropped, not short, but quite dramatically.*)
Time, gentlemen . . . I beg your pardon. Time please,
gentlemen and landgirls for the Republic.
(KATE *gives him the finger.* HARRY *goes off with the glasses.*
KATE *wanders up on to the stage and looks around at the
clothing with gentle disdain. She moves towards the centre of the
stage and opens her mouth to speak.* HARRY *returns, ignores
her, and reaches across to pick up the knickers. He leaves.
Before* KATE *can speak again* TISH *enters, naked under an old
robe or raincoat. She stuffs the school uniform bit by bit into a
Sainsbury's carrier bag. She smiles at* KATE, *who doesn't smile
back, then goes off.* KATE *looks out across the room and tries to
get the feel of the place. She shudders. As she opens her mouth
to speak,* TISH *returns.*)

TISH: Have you seen my knickers?

KATE: Yes. I've seen them stretched across your arse, dangling
from your index finger, and lying on the floor. I've seen
more of your knickers today than I've seen of mine. I
should be very surprised if anyone here five minutes ago
failed to see your knickers. The entire playground's seen
your fucking knickers.
(TISH *gives a strange half-cough, half-sneeze.* HARRY *returns.*)

TISH: Harry, someone's taken my knickers.
(HARRY *hands her a fiver.*)

HARRY: Punter made an offer.

TISH: Who?

HARRY: Some bloke.

TISH: What bloke? Harry, I wish you wouldn't.

(HARRY *winks and leaves with more glasses*.)

Bet your life he got more than this. I once got offered £25 for a pair of fishnets. I do wish he wouldn't, though. I spend enough of my life in Marks and Spencer's as it is.

(TISH *turns to leave*.)

KATE: You do realize that less than a mile from here, about a week ago, a girl younger than us was raped and had some unnameable object thrust so far into her she died. It was done by a man the *Daily Star* is calling The Son of the Ripper. Had you heard?

(*A dog barks downstairs*.)

TISH: Yes.

KATE: She was his fifth victim. Her name was Angela something.

TISH: No, her name was Alison. Excuse me.

(*The dog barks*. TISH *leaves*. HARRY *wanders back*.)

KATE: Harry, we need more light up here.

HARRY: Now don't you go touching it. It's electric.

KATE: I know it's electric; they're electric lights. That means they're supposed to light up. There they all are, Harry. Wouldn't it be absolutely wonderful if they worked? Wouldn't that be amazing? If what was actually there actually worked?

HARRY: Bit less of the cheek young lady, and I might find time to have a look this afternoon. Until then don't touch it. (*He shouts through the door to* TISH.) Help yourself to a drink, princess. Warm yourself up.

TISH: (*Off*) Thanks, Harry.

(HARRY *leaves*. TISH *enters and ignores* KATE. *She helps herself to a large vodka, sits to drink it, and swallows some antihistamines*.)

KATE: I was out of order. I apologize. Did you know her?

TISH: She was with my agent. She did her first gigs with me; I helped her get her act together. She'd only just left home, but she was very good.

KATE: Why do you do it?

TISH: Do what?

KATE: Teeny-bop around with nothing on in front of these appendaged penises.

TISH: Well, my typing speed's a joke.

KATE: I'm serious.

TISH: It got me my Equity card.

KATE: Christ.

(*Pause.* TISH *coughs and sneezes.*)

TISH: What do you do for a living?

KATE: I'm funny.

TISH: Oh. I haven't got a sense of humour.

KATE: I'm not surprised.

(KATE *climbs onstage.*)

TISH: Are you going to be funny now?

KATE: I shouldn't think so. I might be tonight if I manage to get some work done. (*She takes off her jacket.*) Christ. What's it like taking all your clothes off up here?

TISH: It's not like taking them off. I mean you only put them on to take them off again. It's like you never had them on at all.

KATE: But you're a grown woman. Don't you find it humiliating? I find it humiliating enough just watching you. (HARRY *has returned for more glasses.*)

HARRY: You leave her alone. It isn't as easy as it looks, her game. There's an art to it. I've seen a lot of them and, believe me, she's good. You know. There's a simplicity in what she does. She's um . . .

KATE: Simple.

HARRY: She's a nice girl. Don't listen to her; you're a nice girl. If I had any daughters left I'd prefer they entered show business than joined the SAS. She's a nice girl.

(HARRY *exits.*)

KATE: Which bits are the nicest, Harry?

(TISH *coughs.*)

I don't care how nice you are. To do what you do you must be pretty desperate or pretty stupid.

TISH: I saw a thing on TV about how being funny isn't about

being funny at all; it's really about being really, really nasty.

KATE: So?

TISH: You must be really, really funny.

KATE: I'd like to work now, is that OK with you?

TISH: Go ahead.

KATE: Look, I don't think you'd like the act; would you mind fucking off?

(TISH *sneezes*.)

TISH: Well, I was going to stay. I got a stag this evening and nowhere to go in between, so Harry said I could hang around. I don't like to walk the streets round here at the moment.

KATE: Fair enough. (*She steps down from the stage and turns off the main lights so that the coloured lights remain, then climbs back*.) Christ.

TISH: I can't see your face.

KATE: That's because the lights aren't focused on my face. That's because the lights are focused on someone else's tits. (TISH *smiles*. KATE *gets a chair and climbs on it to reach the lights*.)

TISH: Do you know what you're doing?

KATE: Of course I don't know what I'm doing. I had to take four years' fucking cookery. I can make a great victoria sponge. I'll probably make a bloody great victoria sponge of this.

TISH: Is that a joke?

KATE: Yes, that's a joke. Well done.

(KATE *pulls from the wall a length of five by one with spotlights screwed to it. She falls off the chair and the lights go out. They are left in darkness but for a dim glow from somewhere beyond the serving hatch*.)

Oh, bugger.

TISH: I don't like the dark.

KATE: Very helpful.

TISH: Turn the lights on.

KATE: I can't turn the lights on. I am bound hand and foot by the lights.

TISH: I'll turn them on then.

KATE: Don't you bloody dare.

TISH: What shall I do then? Shall I just sit here? What shall
I do?

KATE: Well, for a start stop acting like a fucking woman.
(*As they speak, a figure rises from behind the hatch. It is a tall
figure with a strange, shiny bald head.* KATE *sees it, though it
remains behind* TISH.)
Who's there?

TISH: Me.

KATE: Who is it?

TISH: Me. I'm here.

KATE: Shut up.

TISH: Why?
(*The figure very slowly begins to climb over the bar.*)

KATE: Come here.

TISH: Where?

KATE: Come over here.

TISH: I can't see anything.

KATE: Just get up and come here.

TISH: Why?

KATE: Because there's some fucker behind you!!
(TISH *turns and screams. She runs across the room overturning
a few chairs. The figure disappears from the light. After a few
seconds' silence, the main lights come on. Standing by the light
switch is a tall man wearing a plastic bald head and glasses. He
looks around him, blinking like an owl. It is* NICK, *doing a
remarkably good impersonation of Eric Morecambe.*)

NICK: (*Morecambe*) I'm sorry about that.

KATE: You bastard.

NICK: Is that you, Ern? That is fantastic. Your own mother
wouldn't know you. What are you, a Christmas tree?

KATE: You stupid shit.

NICK: Can she say that?

KATE: You frightened the life out of her.

NICK: (*Turns the bald head around and becomes Kojak*) Who loves
you, baby? Daddy does. Stavros! Lock these broads away
and don't let anybody get at them!

(NICK *exits*.)

KATE: Are you OK?

(TISH *nods and rises in a slight state of shock. She takes an asthma spray from her bag and uses it.*)

I'm sorry. He thinks he's funny. What's wrong?

TISH: Nothing. I'm always like this. I have to go to the loo.

(TISH *leaves.* KATE *prepares to work.* NICK *walks in on his knees doing ET.*)

NICK: Elliot, I go home. Gift for Elliott. (*Elliot*) Oh boy, he's a cute little fella. I'll keep him as a pet. What do I call him? (*ET*) Call him Herpy.

KATE: Do you get *all* your material off toilet walls?

NICK: (*James Stewart*) Katherine, welcome home. I've missed you so damned awfully I could cry. I'm sorry to get emotional. It's just that I love you, Katherine.

KATE: Well, you've got a fucking evil way of showing it.

(*He kisses her.*)

Don't.

NICK: (*De Niro*) Oh come on, hey, what's one little kiss? Kiss gonna kill you?

KATE: Look, I've had time to think and I don't want to get involved again, OK? I don't want my miserable little life entwined with your miserable little life. Or anyone's. It sounds like a cliché, I know, but since I've been away I've learned to be alone and it's the best thing I ever taught myself.

NICK: (*Tom Conti*) It's hard to explain, this being in love. Trying to explain what being in love is like is like trying to explain Day-Glo orange to someone who went blind the week before they invented it. It's so orange you can't imagine, you tell him. I've seen orange, he says. But this is more orange than that, you tell him. Like a Belisha beacon, he says. Like the fruit, orange? No, you say, more orange than orange. That's how I love you.

KATE: Who the fuck was that?

NICK: Tom Conti.

KATE: Nick, that's a bit obscure.

NICK: Yes, but he's very good at sincerity.

(*He kisses her.*)

KATE: And who was that?

NICK: Who would you like?

KATE: Oh no . . .

NICK: Anyone you want, Katey.

KATE: Bastard. (*Pause.*) Robert De Niro.

NICK: No problem.
(*He does a lot of preparation, then kisses her like Robert De Niro.*)

KATE: Not bad. Sean Connery.
(NICK *thinks for a moment.*)

NICK: (*Sean Connery*) OK, let me see now, I've always had a penchant for kissing pussy galore, so if you'd just take your clothes off, Miss Moneypenny. . .

KATE: Nick, that's not funny.
(*He kisses her again, unhurriedly.*)

KATE: Mmm hmm. Richard Pryor.

NICK: Then get your ass over here, motherfucker. Or I'll get my ass over there. (*He kisses her again.*) Macho-man! I put your tongue right down your throat, I'm Macho-man.

KATE: Mick Jagger.

NICK: You old slag. (*He kisses her.*)

KATE: Thank you. No, that's quite enough.

NICK: Nastassia Kinski.

KATE: You'll be lucky.

NICK: My turn! Nastassia Kinski.

KATE: It's your game, not mine.

NICK: Oh, don't be bloody mean. Give us um . . . Isabelle Huppert.

KATE: Get off, you lecherous sod. (*She kisses him anyway.*)

NICK: Who was that?

KATE: Me.

NICK: Oh wow. Big deal.
(*She thumps him.*)

NICK: Your turn.

KATE: You.
(*They look at each other.*)
You.

NICK: ET.

KATE: No, never!

(*They struggle. He pins her down.*)

NICK: Bob Monkhouse.

KATE: Get off me.

NICK: Rowan Atkinson.

KATE: Fucking get off me!!

(*He gets off her.*)

NICK: Prince Charles?

KATE: You.

NICK: Michael Caine.

KATE: I want you. That's all, I just want you.

NICK: John Hurt.

KATE: John Hurt?

NICK: John Hurt.

KATE: OK.

NICK: John Hurt in *The Elephant Man*.

KATE: No!

(*She screams. They fight. The fight turns into a clinch and the clinch into a kiss. They cuddle up to each other.*)

Who's this? Is this you? I don't trust you. Not one little bit.

(TISH *returns, looking great.*)

TISH: Sorry.

NICK: (*Cliff*) Hi.

TISH: Hello.

KATE: This is Nick. This is . . .

TISH: Tish. Um . . . (*Sneezes.*)

NICK: Pleased to meet you. Hi.

TISH: Hello.

(*They look at each other.*)

KATE: Oh shit.

NICK: You what?

KATE: I'd just like to say that if you two ever go to bed together I'll hang myself in both your bathrooms.

NICK: Oh, come on, Kate . . .

TISH: Honestly.

(NICK *and* TISH *look at each other for half a second longer than is diplomatic.* NICK *looks at* KATE *as* TISH *looks away.*

TISH *looks at* KATE *as* NICK *looks away.*)

KATE: Second thoughts, I'll do it straight away.

NICK: Kate, we've only just met. You just introduced us.

KATE: I know. I just don't like to feel I'm standing in anybody's way, that's all.

NICK: Katey, you're completely bloody paranoid.

KATE: I am not paranoid! I am genuinely hated by a great many people. I am regularly done in, shat on and betrayed by my closest friends. If I'm paranoid, Nikki Lauda's a hypochondriac!

(*Enter* HARRY.)

HARRY: (*To* NICK) Right, I've got some bones to pick with you. First, I've had to get in another barman because young Jane won't serve up here no more. She had to say three Hail Marys last week after watching you lot. So I've got an extra man on and you're paying for him.

NICK: Oh, come on, Harry, you know how much we take.

HARRY: I'll go a third.

NICK: Fifty-fifty.

HARRY: All right, fifty-fifty. But I want another interval.

NICK: Harry, if we have another interval there'll be more intervals than acts.

HARRY: You know what's wrong with the new left? Half the buggers drink St Clements and the other half are under the table after one bottle of Pils. If it wasn't for Pernod I'd go bust. Get some beer drinkers in, will you, or I'll cancel you and book in the Women-Only Disco. None of them'd be seen dead with a half-pint glass.

NICK: (*Harry*) All right, Harry. I'll do my best to get them pissed and legless . . .

HARRY: Oh aye, very clever.

NICK: Oh aye.

HARRY: Oh aye.

NICK: Very clever.

HARRY: Oh, and there's a message for you. Some bloke called from Cardiff. Sounded like a coloured chap.

NICK: What'd he say?

HARRY: He said he left his bookings diary at Scotch Corner and was it tonight?

NICK: Yes, it's tonight.

HARRY: How many of them?

NICK: Don't worry, Harry; they're a bit like the Black and White Minstrels.

HARRY: I don't care what colour they are as long as there's no *bloody oildrums*! You're to phone him anyway if he's coming. Fifteen-piece bloody brass bands . . . (*Exit* HARRY.)

KATE: Who are they?

NICK: Bunch of Rastas I saw in Edinburgh.

KATE: Coming from Cardiff?

NICK: Yes. Local band. Ja Cymru.

(NICK *leaves, having found his address book*.)

TISH: Are you and Nick um . . .

KATE: I think the word's entwined.

TISH: But you do have a relationship?

KATE: I wouldn't say that. Trying to make a relationship of what we have is a bit like trying to decorate a trifle after you've thrown it against the wall.

TISH: I see.

KATE: I'm sorry if I was a little premature there, but you're definitely his type.

TISH: How do you mean?

KATE: You're female. I mean, look at you. I can't compete with that. He'll want you, and he usually gets what he wants. It's inevitable.

TISH: Well, perhaps I'll say no.

KATE: Yeah. Look, I haven't done a gig in two months; do you mind if I get on with some work?

TISH: What is it you do exactly?

KATE: I told you. I'm funny. I'm very funny, or at least I was.

TISH: Why was?

KATE: I haven't been around for a while. I don't know if I feel funny any more.

TISH: Why not?

KATE: Well, there are a lot of things in this world that drive me up the wall. I thought if I made fun of them they wouldn't

18

but as it turned out they now drive me up the wall and across the ceiling.

TISH: What things?

KATE: Oh, men in particular. Men in general. Men in TR7s. Men in John Player Special T-shirts. You name it. If I want it, it doesn't want me. If it wants me it's a garden gnome. I've never had a man who didn't do me in.

TISH: Neither have I.

KATE: I got off to a terrible start. I lost my virginity to a Spaniard.

TISH: So did I. So did I.

KATE: I was fourteen.

TISH: That's amazing. So was I.

KATE: I was raped.

TISH: Oh, I'm sorry.

KATE: You needn't be. He was only twelve, and I was on top. It happened, to my eternal shame, in a hotel in Marbella. Where did you find yours?

TISH: School cruise. Five of us decided we'd all lose our virginity by the time we reached Athens. The others all had spotty third formers from Ampleforth. I did much better. I had our waiter. His name was Jaquemo.

KATE: Sounds painfully exotic.

TISH: Well, Daddy was in the Diplomatic so I had my ear nibbled in every country under the sun, when I was younger. I've made love on a beach in Oman, on a night train through Germany, in a shack on stilts in Singapore. You name it. It's not that I'm romantic, I'm just susceptible to environments. I find it awfully hard to say no. I think I've only said no once and that was to Colin Welland. At least he said he was Colin Welland.

KATE: Colin Welland?

TISH: Well, he looked like Colin Welland. That's why I said no. Anyway, he wasn't, he was just this bloke who told everyone he was.

KATE: Jesus. I hate men. I hate, loathe and detest men; no wonder my sex life is awful; I can't stand the bastards. Especially the ones that come up to you and say 'Hello'. I

can't stand it when a man comes up to me and says it like
that. 'Hello.'

(*Enter* KEITH, *carrying part of a PA. He puts it down and
smiles.*)

KEITH: Hi.

KATE: That's close enough.

(KEITH *does a trick. It's quite a good one and* TISH *quite enjoys
it.* KATE *is not in the least impressed.*)

TISH: Oh wow, that's amazing. That's really good.

KATE: I'm astounded.

KEITH: Have I shown you it before?

KATE: No, it was boring the first time.

TISH: How do you do it?

KEITH: Ahah!

KATE: For Christ's sake, Keith, tell her how it's done.

KEITH: It's magic.

KATE: What are you doing here anyway? We don't start until
nine. I want to rehearse, Keith. I haven't done a gig in two
months and everyone and his dog's here. You've got bloody
awful timing and I wish you'd all just fuck off. Hello.

KEITH: How are you?

KATE: Fine.

KEITH: How's Pattie?

KATE: In Brighton.

KEITH: Good to see you.

KATE: Thank you.

(*Pause.*)

KEITH: Do you know anything about this guy from Channel
Four? Supposed to be a guy from Channel Four coming in
tonight.

KATE: Oh yes? Well, if they'd only get themselves organized we
could do them a party booking.

KEITH: Well, you never know, do you?

(*Exit* KEITH.)

KATE: That's Keith.

TISH: A magician.

KATE: I wouldn't go that far. Nick only put him on the bill
because he owns a crappy PA.

20

TISH: He seems nice.

KATE: He's very nice. And he's a prannet.

TISH: I know what you mean. It's easy to like them when they're harmless, isn't it?

(*They both laugh.*)

KATE: Will you stay and watch the show tonight?

TISH: I've got shows myself tonight.

KATE: Well, when I run through, then. Will you listen?

TISH: Why?

KATE: Why not?

TISH: Why me?

KATE: I want to see if I can make you laugh.

TISH: No, you don't. You want to see if you can make me think because you think I don't.

(KATE *laughs.*)

KATE: Fair enough. I wish you were harder to like.

TISH: Why?

(HARRY *backs through the door carrying a toolbox. He finds the lights on the floor.*)

HARRY: Oh, no problem. I see you fixed them.

KATE: Ha ha. Can I use the downstairs bar to work?

HARRY: What's wrong with the next room?

KATE: Nothing Rentokil couldn't deal with.

HARRY: You've made a right bloody mess of this.

(KATE *goes.*)

I'll need my other box. Are you all right, princess?

TISH: Mmm? Yes.

HARRY: Good. You want to watch her, you know. I reckon, don't you?

(*He winks at her and leaves.* TISH *sighs a huge sigh and then sneezes.* NICK *enters and she jumps.*)

NICK: (*Bogart*) How are you doing, honey? My name's Nick.

TISH: I know your name.

NICK: (*Cary Grant*) You're looking a little depressed. I thought being a man of great personality and style I might be able to cheer you up somewhat.

TISH: Who's that? I don't know. I can't tell half of them.

NICK: (*John Wayne*) You want I should make it simple for you?

TISH: Clint Eastwood?

NICK: No.

TISH: Well, who cares, anyway. I don't.

NICK: (*Rik Mayall*) All right. All right. Let's get this sorted
out. Now what on earth's the matter?

TISH: That man from the telly. Thingy.

NICK: (*Rik Mayall*) Well, no, actually.

TISH: Please stop.

NICK: What's wrong?

TISH: You know.

NICK: I don't. What?

TISH: I want you.

NICK: (*Coward*) But, darling, you've already had me.

TISH: I want you again.

NICK: But, Patricia darling, you must be pursued by more men
than Sebastian Coe.

(TISH *tries to touch him. He avoids her.*)

TISH: You said I'd only have to kiss you and you'd want me.

NICK: So?

TISH: So why won't you let me kiss you any more?

NICK: (*Muggeridge*) Things are problematical. Things change.

TISH: Nick . . .

NICK: Look.

TISH: What?

NICK: Kate's back. I don't want to hurt her.

TISH: Why not?

NICK: (*Kenneth Williams*) Because she'll fucking well kill me,
love.

TISH: I wish you'd said.

NICK: If I'd said then we wouldn't know each other as well as
we do now and I think that would be a shame, don't you?

TISH: (*Sneezes.*) I don't know you at all.

NICK: Well, I'm nothing special, am I?

TISH: (*Wipes her nose.*) You made me laugh.

NICK: Well . . . that's my job.

TISH: You lied to me.

NICK: I said exactly what I felt.

TISH: If you don't feel it afterwards I think that's lying.

22

NICK: Well, if I've changed my mind it's not, is it? Be rational for Christ's sake.

(KEITH *enters with the rest of the PA.*)

KEITH: Hi, Nick, how's it going?

NICK: (*Keith*) Hi, Keith, things are great with me, how are things with you?

KEITH: You bastard.

NICK: (*Keith*) You bastard.

KEITH: Is there anyone you can't do?

NICK: Richard Gere. I mean you've got to have something to start with, right?

KEITH: Do you know anything about this Channel Four guy coming in?

NICK: Yeah, apparently he's been sent on a mission to find out what happened to the others.

KEITH: Oh well, you never know.

(KEITH *sets up the PA.* NICK *and* TISH *talk quietly.*)

NICK: Look, I wanted you and I told you I wanted you, that's all.

TISH: It was the way you told me.

NICK: (*Coward*) Very eloquently if I remember rightly. I'm very sorry; I'll give myself a handicap next time. I'll only use phrases like, 'You have lovely eyes; suck this.'

TISH: I'd prefer that to all the rubbish you talked about living for the moment.

NICK: Look, I never lied. I made no promises.

TISH: Yes, you did, whatever you did or didn't say to me you made love to me, and that's a promise.

NICK: Oh, come on . . .

TISH: And you've broken it. You know you have.

(NICK *moves away.*)

NICK: (*To* KEITH) Have you fixed this pile of crap?

KEITH: Yes, it was only I'd left the spare fuse at home.

NICK: Have you got it with you this week?

KEITH: Oh yeah. It's in the amp. Actually, Nick, I've been thinking and I think I need two spots really. I think I need one early on for the escapology and one later on for the magic proper, what do you think?

NICK: Take it from me, Keith, they'd never let you on twice.

KEITH: Nick, do you like my act? No, be honest.

NICK: (*Alexei Sayle*) Well, to be honest, if you want honesty, I'm not exactly in love with you, no. As a matter of fact I only ever wanted you for your PA. I mean you've got a great pair of Ohms, you know what I mean?

(*He glances at* TISH *and leaves.* TISH *and* KEITH *look at each other, embarrassed. Neither can think of anything to say.*

KEITH *is just about to resort to a trick when* HARRY *comes in. He carries a hammer and the evening paper which he throws down on to the table. Beneath the headline 'Face of a Killer?' is an identikit picture of a gaunt man in his late fifties.*)

HARRY: Here he is, then. That's him. I'm not a vindictive man but personally I'd cut his bollocks off. You walk down the street nowadays and a nice pretty girl walks towards you and you look at her legs, you know. It's natural. Or you look at what she's wearing or at her face . . . and then you see it in her eyes. She doesn't trust you. You've never met her, you're never likely to, but you've looked. So as she passes you there's this wave of fear; you can feel it. He's got a lot to bloody answer for. You used to be able to smile at a pretty girl.

KEITH: I think the problem is, Harry, this socket definitely gets overloaded. I've got an extension cable in my Dad's boot; if you've got a two-way adaptor we could bring some wattage in from the next room without blowing the jukebox this time, what do you think?

HARRY: I think if you don't get into your heads this is not the London Palladium somebody's going to die up here.

KEITH: I'll get the extension. It'll be safer in the long run.

(KEITH *goes.* HARRY *begins to repair the lights.*)

HARRY: I'm sorry about your underthings. I thought this time of the year you could do with a little extra cash.

TISH: This time of the year I could do with a little extra clothing.

HARRY: Are you going home for Christmas?

TISH: Oh, I wouldn't be very welcome.

HARRY: I think you should go home. What with this business . . .

TISH: It's all right.

HARRY: It's a nasty business.

TISH: I'll be all right.

HARRY: You better be careful.

TISH: Please, look, I'll be all right.

HARRY: You should go home. Your parents would be pleased to see you.

TISH: My parents aren't exactly proud of me.

HARRY: Do they know where you are?

TISH: Not exactly.

HARRY: I suppose what it is is they don't understand you, right?

TISH: No, they just don't like me. My mother and I only have one thing in common and we both hate him. All the women I've ever known hate men.

HARRY: I've had two wives and three daughters. I drove one to her grave, one to the bottle and the other three out of the house. I am single-handedly to blame for wrecking the lives of five different women and personally responsible for 4,000 years of male domination. Or so I used to be told. There you are. Three daughters.

(*He shows* TISH *a couple of photographs.*)

TISH: What are their names?

HARRY: Regan, Goneril and Lucretia. That's Jennifer, that's Tracey, and that's Paula. She's in California. Tracey's disappeared and Jenny married a man called Frank. You know the type; would never tell you what his job was but drove a Masarati and anything you mentioned could get it for you cheap. She weren't exactly a beauty were Jenny. A lot older than the other two. Paula was always the bright one, and Tracey the pretty one. Jenny took them both in hand when their mother went off to the clinic. She was a good kid, but boring, you know what I mean? Anyway, I'd said to Paula, you're a bright girl, you've got a quick mind, I'm buggered if you're going to waste it. If it costs me a small fortune you're going to secretarial school. And Tracey I thought'd make a good model, you know. Classy stuff like. Or if it turned out she could sing she'd be a damn sight better than some you see on the box; I'd do my best to

25

get her on one of those discovery shows, you know. I know a few people in the business, like. Regulars. I've done them some favours. Anyway, you never know, do you? But Jenny, well, to be quite honest, I don't know what Frank saw in her. Except she had a sweet nature, of course. What I mean is, I'm surprised that meant bugger all to Frank. Anyway, they got wed. Tracey was bridesmaid. Paula on the other hand announced that she didn't believe in marriage or any other form of social oppression and refused to come to the ceremony. I said to her, you're a selfish little cow and if you won't come to your own sister's wedding you can leave this house. I bloody will, she said. So I gave her a backhander and she bloody did. Anyway, Jenny got wed on a wet Thursday down the Paddington registry and we came back here to celebrate. I didn't feel much like celebrating; I had to give this Frank my own tie two minutes before the ceremony. He seemed to think he was nipping in to back a horse. But my thinking was Jenny's mother'd feel bad enough there was no church service; she'd spin in her bloody grave if there was no reception either. Our people made a good show considering; dozen of them came down in a minibus. Pissed out of their brains before they got here. His side of the family was a right shambles, though; some batty old aunt who'd read about it in the local paper and a couple of bloody wide-boy mates of his with their so-called girlfriends. I'd put two hundred quid in the till; soon as that ran out they buggered off. Our lot enjoyed themselves though, it would have been a good night.

TISH: What happened?

HARRY: Oh, there was a run on Scotch so I came up here to get some more. Frank was up here. Jenny, bless her heart, was downstairs knee-deep in non-stick frying pans and Frank's up here with our Tracey. They were on that table, at least she was, with her blue satin frock up round her waist. I felt sick. I said to her, 'That's it. You're out. I'm finished with you.' 'He made me,' she said. 'He made me.' Did he, buggery. I gave her the back of my hand. I hadn't hit that

26

girl for years. And this Frank, this son-in-law of mine, didn't lift a bloody finger. He just watched.

TISH: Didn't you hit him?

HARRY: He weren't worth the trouble. I went downstairs and told Jenny. I was buggered if I was going to leave her in ignorance. His car was outside; his mates had covered it in shaving cream. Jenny were sat in a corner. He came down and just started drinking again. They were going to drive down to Brighton for the night, so eventually Jenny got up and she took him round the bar into the parlour. It was noisy in here but I could hear them arguing. Jenny had a mouth on her at times. Then I heard her hit the floor. I was in there like lightning; he'd hit her.

I said, you evil bastard, get out of my pub. I'd have had him that time if my brother Charlie hadn't held me off. But suddenly Jenny's shouting, 'Look, go away . . . go away and leave us alone!' And Charlie dragged me out. Ten minutes later I looked back in and there they are. He's on the floor with her, and she's cradling his head in her arms. And this hand of his is on her knee, with a flashy gold ring on it, and Jenny's ear bleeding where it caught her. Like babes in the bloody wood. So I said, 'If you go with him, you go for ever.' She went. So . . . Jenny's married to a man who'll bring her nowt but misery; Paula's in California; and Tracey, I've no idea. So don't ask me about women. Every woman I've known it always got to the point where all I could do was ignore them or thump them. In the end it always seemed best to part company.

TISH: I don't think you understand women much.

HARRY: That's what they tell me. All my life women have told me I don't understand women. Well, you're wrong. Tell you the truth, the only thing I don't understand about women is what the bloody hell they see in us.

(HARRY *completes his work.* KATE *enters, followed by* NICK.)

KATE: Right, I don't care if you stay or piss off. I want to use the stage. Keith! I'm getting nervous about this. Christ, the last gig I did was a Tuesday night in Chiswick.

(*Enter* KEITH.)

27

KEITH: What?

KATE: Sit.

(KEITH *sits, as do the others.* KATE *changes the lights.*)

KATE: (*To* NICK) Will you tell me if this is funny? I really need to know.

NICK: (*Bilko*) How many times do I have to tell you? You're funny, funny, funny. All right, snap to it; let's hear the funny material!

(KATE *takes off her sweater and as she drops it goes into a brief reverie. She snaps herself out of it quickly.*)

KATE: Well, introduce me then.

NICK: OK, OK. (*Prince Charles*) Ladies and gentlemen, or should I say gentlemen and wimmin, which I believe is the popular term for the ones with tits nowadays . . . I'm very honoured to introduce a young lady who has found much favour already in my brother's eyes since he personally awarded her the Duke of Edinburgh Platinum Award for spending four nights under canvas and royalty. My wife Diana, who unfortunately can't be with us tonight as she's home getting pregnant, has called our next act the best entertainment she's had since Sardines at Balmoral when Andrew showed her all the secret passages she never knew were there . . .

KATE: Nick!

NICK: (*Saville*) All right. All right, sensation seekers, we now have for you, live and alone on stage, blah de blah de blah . . . few big laughs at your expense and uppity women in general . . . blah de blah de blah . . . Kate Kelvin!

(KATE *strides into the spotlight.*)

KATE: Wotcher, kids! (*Pause.*) You remember the first time your parents took you to the theatre, to the panto? The star would come on; Arthur Askey or Norman Vaughan; it was always a man and he was always dressed as a woman, and he'd shout, 'Wotcher, kids!' And if it was Norman Vaughan we'd all shout back, 'Fuck off!' So I'm going to go off and come back on again and I'll shout, 'Wotcher, Kids!' and you all shout, 'Fuck off!' Right?

HARRY: Lights OK for you now, are they?

KATE: Fuck off. (*Starts again.*) Wotcher, kids. (*Pause.*) Oh
Christ. Beam me up, Scotty. Let's try again, shall we? And
answer this time or I'll chuck liquorice allsorts at you. And
get three of you up to sing a little song about ducks and
give you so many presents you'll drop them all over the
stage and burst into tears . . . Oh, God how I hate Norman
Vaughan. One more time. 'Wotcher, kids!' (*Dull response.*)
Look, your Dad's not sitting next to you now; you can let
rip, you're grown-ups. I mean I wish you could see
yourselves. There's a bloke sitting there – (*Imitates him.*)
'I think people are going to shout this time; perhaps I'd
better shout after all. Are more people going to shout or not
shout I wonder; I'd rather do what everyone's going to do. I
know . . . I'll shout without moving my lips. As long as
everyone else does . . . Fuck off!' And there's another man
here in the front row, 'I'm not going to shout; I paid four
quid.' Quite right, too. One more time. 'Wotcher, kids!'
It's getting worse. Forget it.

I'm here to tell you what the problem is for women. The
problem for women in general, and female comedians in
particular, but generally the problem for women is they
can't piss in public and maintain their dignity at the same
time. For men, pissing in public is probably the most
dignified thing they can do, you know? (*She imitates some
very cocky public pissing.*) But women. Forget it. It's all
nettle stings and weeing on your knickers, right? And it's a
big problem for me, especially. Lenny Bruce, he came to
England thirty years ago and he took a slash on the drapes
and he became famous. He became a hero. Can you imagine
what a prick I'd look?

I can see we've got a critic here; he wrote down the
reference to Lenny Bruce. You going to mention Lenny
Bruce in a column about me? I'm very flattered. I'm
deeply, deeply flattered. He's going to look down and piss
all over you, but I'm deeply flattered. Lenny Bruce was OK
in my books. As racist, sexist, Jewish men go, he was OK.
NICK: He was a fuck sight better than you!
(*Pause.*)

I'm heckling. I'm heckling.

KATE: All right. All right. What did you say?

NICK: I said Bruce was a better comedian than you are.

KATE: Yes, well I'm a better fuck. No, that's dreadful.

NICK: Go for the throat.

KATE: OK. OK. That's a very nice suit you're wearing, sir. I hear they're very fashionable. Again.

NICK: Heard it before. Very boring.

KATE: Look, I'm trying to concentrate, so just shut the fuck up.

NICK: Oh, very witty.

KATE: Shut up! Let's discuss this later; perhaps at your parents' wedding. For the moment I'm talking and I'd like to talk about fucking.

I like to talk about fucking because thanks to the kind of men I meet I find talking about it much more stimulating than doing it most of the time. Don't get me wrong; I'm not frigid. There are times I'll fuck anything, so long as it's vegetable or mineral. You know what I mean? Did you ever have one of those weekends on your own when you just can't stop? I do. I have fucked everything in our house. You name it, it has given me pleasure. I mean, after all it's more enjoyable with inanimate objects. You don't have to tell a shower hose you thought he was great. And you don't have to make coffee for them and you don't have to make funny little squeaking noises for them either. 'Oooohoh. . . !' There's no pretence. You don't have to pretend bugger-all for a shampoo bottle. If it's not doing anything for you you don't have to encourage it, you just put it back on the shelf. Shampoo won't give a shit. It's not going to give you the third degree, you know?

'I know you're fucking something else, don't ask me how, I can just feel it in my deep-down cleanser. Who are you fucking?'

'No one. Nothing. Don't get yourself in a lather.'

'Don't lie to me.'

'All right. All right. I admit it. I fucked the telephone.'

'The telephone? How could you fuck the telephone?'

'Look, I fucked it once. Once. I was drunk and it just

30

happened, that's all.'

'What's the telephone do for you that I can't do for you?'

'The telephone talks to me. You never talk to me.'

'I'm a shampoo bottle; I'm not good with words. Who else have you been with?'

'No one else.'

'Who else?'

'OK. You know that little appliance for doing the corners on the stairs that fits into the vacuum cleaner. . . ? We had a thing together. But it was before I even bought you.'

'You never really loved me at all, did you?'

'Look, I like you. I'll always like you. You're good for my hair; I get a really nice shine with you, but you just don't turn me on any more.'

'You're a real bitch. Try washing your hair with the telephone or the vacuum cleaner; see how well they treat you. And let me tell you something for your own good; that little appliance for doing the stairs; there's nowhere he hasn't poked himself . . .'

You get none of that. The nice boy in the front row is looking a little confused. That was a routine about masturbation. We do it too but we don't go blind. We don't even close our eyes.

You know, I never could work out how to discover, how to find out, if the person you're about to sleep with; the person you are about to allow entrance to your body; how do you find out if the bastard's got any killer diseases? You've got his thing in your hand and nothing better to do; you'd quite like to fuck him, so what do you say to make sure?

'Er, before we go any further, have you got any killer diseases? Are you going to hide little murderers in my spine?'

You can't ask someone that. Even someone with a very suspicious-looking thing. What you have to do is, you have to wait until the very last moment, and just before he enters you you say, 'Be careful, I might be a bit sore.'

Then he'll stop. I guarantee he'll stop. And he'll casually

ask you who you've been sleeping with . . . do you sleep around . . . And if you've got any killer diseases! And you can say, 'Of course not, you suspicious-minded reprobate! Why, have you?' 'No!' he'll say. 'A lot of my friends have had it since I came back from New York, but I'm fine, I'm fine.'

Oh, the panic. It's serious, yes? Free love's dead, then. Monogamy's back. Big joke. That's it. That's the new stuff.

(KATE *turns the lights back on.*)

HARRY: That your idea of humour, is it?

KATE: Yes.

HARRY: Not funny though, is it?

KATE: No, it isn't really.

(KATE *corners* NICK.)

Well? Do you think it's funny? Do you think I'm funny?

NICK: No, but you are a great fuck.

HARRY: Hey, language!

(HARRY *exits.*)

KATE: Thanks, that's very encouraging.

KEITH: I thought it was fantastic. Really. Fantastic.

KATE: Fuck off.

(KEITH *fiddles with his PA.*)

Nick?

NICK: Derivative. It's not you up there yet. It's Richard Pryor with tits.

KEITH: Actually, I've been thinking. I think I'll trade in these Ohms and get a couple of Bose. I mean it's only money, isn't it? What do you think?

NICK: How about another mike?

KEITH: How about another spot?

NICK: How about getting off my back?

KATE: What shall I do then? What shall I do?

NICK: Just be you, right?

(NICK *leaves,* KEITH *follows him.*)

KEITH: It's no big deal, it's just I get them warmed up and then I'm off, you know . . .

(*He leaves.* KATE *sits at* TISH's *table.*)

KATE: Well?

TISH: Oh, it was lovely. It was really good.

KATE: You hated it.

TISH: No, really, it was . . .

KATE: Dreadful.

TISH: No, well . . . it wasn't really what . . .

KATE: What did you hate about it?

TISH: Well, I don't know, but I suppose . . . Look, I liked it.

KATE: You're a little liar! What did you bloody well think?

TISH: Well, I found it a bit offensive actually.

KATE: Oh, you found it offensive?

TISH: I don't know. A bit.

KATE: You found it obscene?

TISH: Well, no . . .

KATE: That which offends is obscene.

TISH: All right then, I don't know. Obscene.

KATE: As in pornographic?

TISH: I don't know.

KATE: It's the same thing!

TISH: Is it?

KATE: Yes.

TISH: All right then, it was pornographic.

(KATE *gets up.*)

KATE: Then I don't know why I bother. I should leave it to you, I suppose. You're obviously the more entertaining of the two of us.

TISH: No. You were very good. It's just I didn't really understand the jokes.

KATE: The jokes aren't the point. You're meant to listen to what I'm saying. Did you hear a thing I said?

TISH: I don't know. I was waiting for a joke.

(*Enter* NICK.)

NICK: The call box is knackered. I've got to go home and call these bloody Welshmen. Do you want a cup of coffee?

KATE: Yeah, OK. I'll get my coat.

(KATE *leaves.*)

NICK: Look, I'd like to see you again but Kate and I have got this thing . . . you know how things are.

TISH: She's going to hate me, isn't she? First she'll hate us both, then she'll love you again and just hate me. That's not fair.

NICK: She's not going to hate you because she's not going to
know. Look, there's no reason we can't be friends.
(KATE *returns. Exit* NICK. KATE *calls* TISH's *attention to the
newspaper lying on the table.*)

KATE: I'm sorry, but you said you knew her. Don't you
understand why she died? Because she was available.
Because women like you make yourselves available. They're
killing us now for sport. One man rips us up so the rest of
them can read about it; get a little pang of feeling in their
cocks under the breakfast table. It's a thirst. And you think
I perform pornography?

TISH: I never said that.

KATE: That's the trouble! You've got nothing to say. You've got
to work out what you hate about this shitty place and then
do something about it. And the first thing to do is break
silence. Say what you think. Say something. Do something.

TISH: Umm . . .

KATE: For her at least. Something.
(*Exit* KATE. *Enter* HARRY.)

HARRY: I have to go now; couple of frames. I'll have to lock up
the place around you as usual. You be all right until five
thirty?

TISH: Yes.

HARRY: Don't drink too much.

TISH: Yes.

HARRY: Be good, princess.

TISH: Harry?

HARRY: Yes?

TISH: What do you think when you watch me work? Do you
ever get any funny ideas? You know?

HARRY: Me? No. Not guilty.
(*He looks at her and then leaves.* TISH *listens as the doors
below are slammed and locked. The dog barks, then there is
quiet. Over a long period,* TISH *becomes jumpy and frightened.
This causes her to sneeze and scratch and makes her breathing
more and more difficult. Upset with herself, she takes out some
tablets to help her sneezing. Slowly she makes a little collection
of bottles on the table of everything from aspirin to Haliborange.*

34

She pours herself a large vodka and a glass of water and returns to her table. She begins slowly to take the tablets. We watch her move into a slow routine of swallowing. We watch her take at least three dozen tablets.
The lights fade.)

ACT TWO

The same. TISH'*s eyes are closed. Her head nods and jerks a few times. When she finally falls asleep her head hits the table with a bang and she wakes. She sees the jars and bottles in front of her as if for the first time. Like a naughty child she hides the mess by sweeping it into her bag. The moment of panic gives way to her tiredness and she begins to nod off again, but there is fear now. The dog barks loudly downstairs. The darker it becomes for her, the less she wants it to grow dark.* KEITH *enters.*

KEITH: Hi. Have you got a minute? Can I show you something? It's one I haven't tried yet.
(TISH *can't fathom what's happening. She just stares at him.*)
You look knackered. Are you OK?
(*Pause.* TISH *sighs and looks confused.*)
Sorry, were you asleep? I'm sorry, I'll go away.
(KEITH *turns to go.* TISH *discovers an empty bottle in her hand, remembers what she's done, and jumps up to stop him. She's afraid, but too far gone to speak. Another impasse.*)
I used to just do it for fun as a kid but I thought, well, why not give it a go? It's still very popular, magic. Vavoom!
(*He does an impression of Tommy Cooper that almost makes her fall over.*)
Sorry.
(*He turns to go again.* TISH *grabs him and pushes him into the middle of the room, then sits herself on a chair in front of him. She has difficulty focusing but convinces him she wants to watch.*)
Right, um . . . OK. This is a new thing I've been working on, so don't watch too carefully. (*Pause.*) Er, I'm not quite ready; could you close your eyes for a moment?
(TISH *shakes her head as it is an unwise suggestion.*)
It's not cheating; there's always some preparation. It's just that I don't have a leggy assistant to make you look over there. (*He points. She looks.*) No, I mean, er . . . Could you just cover your eyes up for a second?

36

(*She covers her eyes. He pops a billiard ball into his mouth.
This makes it impossible for him to tell her to open her eyes.
He removes the ball.*)

OK, you can open them now.

(*She opens and focuses. This makes it impossible for him to
return the ball to his mouth.*)

Sorry, look, could you just close them again and er, count
to five and open them? Sorry.

(*She closes her eyes. He puts the ball in his mouth. He stands
like a magician and waits. And waits. She doesn't open her eyes
because she has fallen asleep. Eventually he removes the ball.*)

OK.

(*And pops it back in again quickly.* TISH *doesn't respond, so
eventually he taps her on the shoulder. She rouses and focuses
once more. He smiles and stands like a magician. As he is about
to start the trick . . .*)

TISH: What's your name again?

(*He is banjaxed once more. He coughs a quick ingenious cough
and spits out the ball into his hand, where he palms it.*)

KEITH: My name's Keith. I know, I know. But I find it works
to my advantage, like a boy named Sue, you know?

(TISH *feels herself drowsing.*)

TISH: Keith?

KEITH: Are you sure you're all right?

TISH: Would you show me this trick, please?

KEITH: Sure. OK. Er . . . What's that up there?

(*He points in the air to misdirect her. She stares at him
steadfastly.*)

Up there!

(*She still stares straight at him.*)

You're making this very difficult, you realize that.

(*Suddenly he dashes around her, putting the ball in his mouth
on the way round. She loses him entirely for a moment, then
focuses on him again. He stands like a magician, she sits like a
rabbit in headlights. He does the trick, producing half a dozen
balls from his mouth, a few from his ears, multiplying and
vanishing them, finally producing a ball from her ear, a lemon
from his own, and a grapefruit from God knows where.* TISH *is*

the best audience he's ever had. She remains glued to every
move, and when the trick is over, she stays glued.)
Da-da! I thank you.
(*She can't respond yet.*)
I really think you could do with some sleep. Why don't you
get your head down . . .

TISH: No, please . . .

KEITH: Oh no, I'm sorry. I never tell anyone how they're done.
It's magic.
(KEITH *leaves.* TISH *gets up, goes behind the bar, and throws*
up. From below the sound of doors being unlocked. TISH *sits*
down and composes herself. KATE *enters, followed by* NICK.)

NICK: (*Richard Burton*) It's very easy really. You see, you put
your lips together and pop some air out and you get a puh,
or a buh, or you can use your tongue and get a duh or a cuh
or a guh and then if you keep your mouth open and change
the shape of your lips about you can get vowels like eee or
aaa or ooo; and then you put them all together; puh, duh,
guh, eee, aaa, ooo, and e-vent-u-a-lly you find-you-
can-make-words. And if you put the words together that
means you can speak and if you do it with other human
beings it's called talking to each other and is generally
recognized as a very good thing.
(KATE *sits silently. She gives him a black look.*)
So talk to me.

KATE: Fuck off.

NICK: (*Michael Caine*) Did you know that the human brain is
fifty times superior to that of any other species; that there
are nearly two dozen tiny muscles and ligaments in the jaw
alone, and all you can come up with is . . .

KATE: Nick, please. Give it a rest.
(*He shrugs and leaves.*)
Are you all right?
(TISH *nods.*)
I've said some pretty shitty things. I'm sorry. It's nothing
personal. I upset people for a living. As a matter of fact I
quite like you, OK?

TISH: Thank you.

KATE: Do you like me?

TISH: No.

KATE: Well, fuck you then.

TISH: Not much.

(*She smiles.* KATE *smiles.*)

KATE: You're not in a very good state, are you? I'm sorry about your friend.

(TISH *sneezes violently, then begins to cry.*)

Look, I'm no good with . . . Oh, go on then. It'll do you good. I don't know why, but they say it does.

TISH: I'm all right. I just wish . . . I wish we could bury her. They won't let us. They have to keep her, like some sort of evidence or something. I wish we could bury her.

KATE: For what it's worth, when my Dad died I kept telling myself I'd feel different after the funeral. He was cremated in Barnes. It's what he wanted. Well, he didn't stipulate Barnes. Anyway, I didn't feel different at all, except that it felt like Sunday all day, but it wasn't. She's gone, so you just have to let her go.

TISH: I'm scared.

KATE: Well, so am I.

TISH: But I'm scared of everybody.

KATE: Well, at least now we know what he looks like. Only about seven million men in the country fit the description. He's tall, apparently, and gaunt. In his fifties.

TISH: I know. I was the one who described him.

KATE: Jesus.

TISH: This one man would turn up wherever Alison was playing. He was besotted. She got quite fond of him, chatted. I saw them leave together that night. I don't know, he might not have. It could have been anyone. I shouldn't be telling you this. Don't say anything.

(KEITH *comes on with a variety of ropes and a pair of handcuffs.*)

KEITH: You know you really don't look well. I think you've got what I had last week.

TISH: I'm all right. Excuse me.

KEITH: There's this herbal stuff called EPC. It's great.

(TISH *leaves.*)

39

Nick's practising his Woody Allen. I wish I was Woody Allen.

KATE: Don't be silly, Keith. What's Woody Allen got that you haven't?

KEITH: Diane Keaton, Charlotte Rampling, Mia Farrow, Mariel Hemmingway. And a Jewish mother. I want a Jewish mother.

KATE: Believe me, they're overrated.

KEITH: Would you help me with this?

(*He gestures to the ropes and handcuffs. During the scene he will get* KATE *to tie and handcuff him to a chair.*)

I suppose what I really want is to come clean.

KATE: How do I do this?

KEITH: Tight. Tighter.

KATE: What do you mean, come clean?

KEITH: Well, it's a bit rehearsed, I suppose.

KATE: What?

KEITH: Well, it's quite hard to say because I don't know how much you realize. About the way I feel about you.

(*Pause.* KATE *pulls a rope around him tightly.*)

Had you realized?

KATE: Yes, I suppose so. I had really, I suppose.

KEITH: So I'm coming clean.

(*Pause. She carries on tying.*)

I might get a bit nervous now.

KATE: No, you won't.

KEITH: I usually do.

KATE: Well, don't.

(*Pause. She comes close to him in the course of tying.*)

God, life's cruel. Thank you for telling me.

KEITH: I wanted you to know at least. I'm quite together about it, don't worry. If it's a big no just say so. I'm not the sort of frog that gets bigger the longer you refuse to kiss it. I don't want it to get in the way of any friendship we may have, I just think you should know I'd like to sleep with you. I mean I'd love it. And if that feeling's a secret it can mess things up, so it's best that you know, then I know you know, you know?

KATE: I'm very flattered.

KEITH: That's a no if ever I heard one. Don't worry, I didn't expect a yes.

KATE: I'm sorry. I wish it could be. If I was someone else and could say, well, we like each other so what the hell, come home tonight, I would. But I'm not. I'm me, and I can't do that. You're very charming. A dreadful magician but very charming and I suppose I like it when you're around but I just don't fancy you.

KEITH: Aaaargh! That's it. That's what you shouldn't have said. My stomach just imploded.

KATE: Look, Keith, I'm sorry. I know how it feels. Believe me I know how it feels in there. But I find it hard to believe I'm the cause of it.

KEITH: Helen of Troy kept saying that. Handcuff me. Don't worry, I'll survive. I shall pretend we did and it was awful.

KATE: I don't want you to imagine that.

KEITH: Why not?

KATE: Because it fucking well wouldn't be. If we did. But we're not going to.

KEITH: Gag me, will you?

KATE: How are your insides?

KEITH: What insides? Did you know Houdini could get out of any combination of ropes and cuffs in thirty seconds?

KATE: Well, I wish you the best of luck.

(*She has gagged him and now closes the cuffs.*)

Go.

(*She looks at her watch and waits thirty seconds.* KEITH *struggles like mad for fifteen of them, then settles down to a more concentrated effort.*)

Do you mind if I get on with something else?

(*She sits down with a pad and biro.* NICK *enters with a cardboard cut-out of Thatcher, which he begins to fix up. Then he puts it aside, sits opposite* KATE *and looks at her steadily for some time.*)

NICK: Well?

KATE: What?

NICK: Well what? What's wrong?

KATE: Nothing.

NICK: Oh, come on.

(KATE *looks over at* KEITH.)

Talk to me.

KATE: Well, aren't you the least bit interested?

NICK: In what? What do you mean?

KATE: I've been to Brighton.

NICK: I know you've been to Brighton. If you spent more time working . . .

KATE: Ask me what I've been doing. Ask me what I did in Brighton.

NICK: What did you do in Brighton?

KATE: I got rid of our child.

(*Pause.*)

NICK: (*Kirk Douglas*) You mean you . . . had an abortion?

KATE: No, I left her at my mother's. Christ.

NICK: (*Woody Allen*) Look, er, I always think that, er, there are only two things worth doing before you die, and neither of them . . .

KATE: Nicholas!

NICK: Look, I never said I was capable of looking after a kid! I made it perfectly clear it was the wrong time in my life.

KATE: Well, me too. So I've taken her to my mother's, God help the kid. But I'm not deserting her. I'll return to Brighton when she's fourteen and help her rebel; I'll be the sort of influence I never had when I was a child. Oh God, my mother. Well, who knows, perhaps even my mother's a better bet than I am. Anyway, so there's no kid around any more. Satisfied? Just you and me, hon.

NICK: (*Bogart*) Sure, kid, and this time it'll all be different.

KATE: All Pattie would do in Brighton; she wouldn't respond to me, except to hit my knee as hard as she could with her little fists and shout, 'Naughty girl.' All day long, 'Naughty girl.'

NICK: Well, she always was a bright kid.

KATE: She'll be happier. I know it. My God, she's got the entire fucking ocean down there.

NICK: We'll visit.

KATE: You're joking.

42

NICK: Next weekend.

KATE: Seriously? Would you?

NICK: Kate, I'm not a complete bastard.

KATE: Yes, you are. But you do try, I suppose.

NICK: (*Basil Fawlty*) Basically I am a trying bastard, yes.
(*He grabs her suddenly and kisses her. It always works.*
KEITH's *chair falls over.*)

KATE: Whoops a daisy. Is that part of it?

KEITH: (*Gagged*) Oh, of course.

NICK: Actually you know, this is a better act than your other
one.
(NICK *puts his arm around* KATE. KEITH *looks away and
struggles on.*)

KATE: Just one thing, though. If we're going to be friends then
just be straight with me, OK? Just don't betray me, huh?
I've gotten used to most of the shit you put me through but
I never get used to that.

NICK: (*Tom Conti*) Would I lie to you? (*Himself*) OK.

KATE: You promise?

NICK: I promise.

KATE: I really wish I didn't.

NICK: What?

KATE: Nothing.
(*Enter* TISH. *Everyone smiles at everyone else.* TISH *sits,* KATE
returns to her writing, and NICK *proceeds to hang Thatcher
from the neck above the stage.*)

TISH: If you're all busy, perhaps I should go . . .

KATE: No, stay. Please. Please.
(*Pause.* TISH *settles.*)
(*To* NICK) Have you ever heard a woman say cunt?

NICK: (*Eric Morecambe*) Pardon?

KATE: Cunt. I don't think I've heard a woman say it. Why is
that?

NICK: (*James Stewart*) Well, perhaps they never met you.

KATE: Ha ha. It's a good word. Cunt. It's strong.

NICK: It's awfully rude.

KATE: It is since your lot got hold of it. Cunt. Cunt. Fanny;
yuk. Whatsit, quim.

TISH: I really think I'd better go.

KATE: Don't be ridiculous; it's snowing. Orifice! No, we've all got those.

NICK: What do you want, words for cunt?

KATE: Yes, maybe.

NICK: Bush. Hole. Honeypot.

KATE: Honeypot? Jesus.

NICK: Minge. Mound of Venus.

KATE: God, the mind of man.

NICK: Doughnut. Love box. Beaver.

KEITH: (*Gagged*) Vagina.

KATE: I thought you said it should take about thirty seconds.

KEITH: (*Gagged*) I said it took Houdini thirty seconds.

NICK: The Sulphurous Pit. Crotch. Slit.

TISH: I'm sorry, I really do have to go.
 (*She rises.*)

KATE: No, please. What's wrong?

TISH: I'm sorry, I don't understand why you have to use words like that. They're not particularly funny.

KATE: We were thinking aloud. I'm sorry. Please, sit down.
 (TISH *sits.*)

NICK: Oyster.

KATE: Shut up. I've got it anyway.

TISH: I suppose you think I'm a bit of a prude, I suppose I am. It's just the way I was brought up.

KATE: How were you brought up?

TISH: (*Smiles.*) My mother was a Catholic.

KATE: Ahah! All is explained. You were thrown to the nuns.

TISH: Twelve years in convent school.

KATE: Sounds worse than B'nai Hakiba.

TISH: It was awful. For years I had to put my dressing gown on first and then get undressed for bed; which is actually impossible.
 (KATE *laughs.*)

KATE: Someone should start a club for all those people brought up to believe in God who, as a direct result, don't. Nick's father's a vicar, he can join.

TISH: What about you?

KATE: I'm a life-member. I survived Leviticus. At sixteen I
    knew nothing about contraception and all there is to know
    about leprosy. My idea of rebellion was to be under the
    covers with a torch reading the New Testament.

TISH: I remember in my last year at school I was chosen to play
    Gabriel. It was the best part. So the night before I curled
    my hair. The next morning Sister Mary dragged me up to
    the front of the class and pulled my hair and said I wasn't
    allowed to play Gabriel; I had to play the ox. She said,
    'Angels don't show off!' I thought there's not much point
    being an angel then, really.

KATE: I wish you wouldn't.

TISH: What?

KATE: You keep making me laugh. I'm supposed to be the
    funny one. You're supposed to be the dumb pretty one.

TISH: Sorry.

KATE: Don't be.

TISH: All right.

    (*They smile at each other.*)

NICK: Look, um . . . anyone want to come and play in the
    snow?

KATE: Play in the snow?

KEITH: (*Gagged*) It's no good. I give up. Can someone help me
    out of this?

NICK: Sure. (*Looks at his watch.*) It's half-past six. Come on,
    Kate. Snowballs.

KATE: It's dark; you're crazy.

NICK: Come on.

KATE: All right. But not down the neck. Tish?

TISH: No.

KATE: Oh, come on.

TISH: I've got a bit of a cold.

KATE: Five minutes.

NICK: She's got a cold.

KATE: All right. It's just you and me, ratface. Hey, what
    happened?

NICK: What?

KATE: I'm happy. I'm happy.

45

(NICK *and* KATE *leave. After a pause,* KEITH *tries to smile.*)

KEITH: (*Gagged*) Could you help me out of this, please?

    (TISH *crosses to help* KEITH.)

TISH: Oh, I'm sorry. What do I do?

KEITH: (*Inaudible*) Handcuffs.

    (TISH *tries the cuffs.*)

TISH: Where's the key?

KEITH: Well, do the gag first.

TISH: Sorry.

    (*She undoes the gag. He sticks out his tongue. On the end of it is the key.*)

TISH: What's it doing in there?

KEITH: That's where you keep it.

TISH: Why?

KEITH: To do the trick.

TISH: How?

KEITH: I'm not sure. Perhaps you're meant to swallow it and wait a couple of days.

    (*Pause.* TISH *sneezes.*)

    Bless you.

TISH: Thank you.

    (*She sneezes again.*)

KEITH: Would you like a handkerchief?

TISH: No, thank you.

KEITH: Actually this isn't an ordinary handkerchief.

TISH: Isn't it?

KEITH: No, actually it's haunted.

TISH: I see.

    (KEITH *does the haunted handkerchief trick.* TISH *laughs.*)

    That's very good.

KEITH: I'm glad you laughed. I don't think tricks should be taken too seriously, you know what I mean?

TISH: Do it again.

KEITH: No. No. Sorry.

TISH: Please. Another one then.

KEITH: All right, all right. Well, there's one that's a bit silly. It involves us making a bet together. I bet you . . . um . . .

TISH: What?

KEITH: No.

TISH: No, go on, what?

KEITH: Well, I bet you I can kiss you without touching you. I bet you a pound.

TISH: Why?

KEITH: It's a trick. I bet you a pound I can kiss you without touching you.

TISH: What do you mean? Where?

KEITH: On the lips.

TISH: You'd touch me on the lips.

KEITH: No. I'll kiss you on the lips but I won't touch you anywhere.

TISH: Not even the lips?

KEITH: No touching at all.

TISH: That's impossible.

KEITH: It's a trick.

TISH: You bet me a pound you can kiss me without touching me? Anywhere?

KEITH: Yes.

TISH: What's the catch?

KEITH: Well, never mind if you don't want to . . .

TISH: No, I'm intrigued. All right, I bet you a pound.

KEITH: Right. OK. OK. Right. Now you have to sit perfectly still. You mustn't move. Lift your head up and close your eyes.

TISH: I'll keep my eyes open if you don't mind.

KEITH: All right. Ready?

TISH: I suppose so.

(*He kisses her. It's a gentle kiss but shocks her. She pulls away. He hands her a pound.*)

KEITH: Worth every penny.

(*She turns her head away sadly. Aware and concerned that he may have hurt her feelings, he turns her head back to him. He kisses her again. This time she doesn't pull away.* KATE *returns for her coat.*)

KATE: Have you two been introduced? Tish, this is Keith, Keith this is Tish. Keith's an old friend of mine who's harboured a deep affection for me for some time. In fact just earlier on he was telling me how much he could do with getting his leg over at the moment. You slimey toe-rag. I almost fell for that shit. At least most men are straightforward bastards, but Christ, the arsenal of lies and smarm some of you bring out when you're desperate . . .

KEITH: Kate, we were only . . .

KATE: I couldn't give a fuck. Go on; if the old friends let you down try for a quick one with some little dip who doesn't know any better. Jesus.

KEITH: Look, I meant what I said earlier . . .

KATE: You didn't mean a fucking word and even if you did, what do I care. I said no. I said no to you, you boring little fart and if you were the last wimp on earth the answer would still be no. No! Never! You are out of the running.

KEITH: Look, I kissed her because she's pretty. It's easy to fancy her. It's not easy to fancy you, I know that. I'm confused.

KATE: How many women have you had, Keith?

KEITH: Why?

KATE: How many?

KEITH: Seven.

KATE: And however many you do have, you will always know the number.

KEITH: Well, if you're worried about being a statistic I'm surprised you still see so much of him. He keeps a list of the women he's had. It's enormous. And I shouldn't be surprised if he's started a separate column for the names of your close friends. And your not-so-close friends.

(TISH *coughs, then sneezes.*)

KATE: Already?

KEITH: I shouldn't have said anything, I'm sorry.

(KEITH *leaves.* TISH *sneezes again. As the scene continues she gradually declines into quite a bad asthma attack.*)

KATE: I don't know why I'm surprised. I mean there have been a few. There was a script editor from the BBC called Carol, there was a freelance who interviewed him for *City Limits*, there was Miss Portsmouth nineteen seventy-something;

48

that was quite a big deal. There was some teenager from Webber Douglas and two or three Assembly Room groupies at the Festival this year, and the daughter of a Conservative front-bencher, and my friend Jenny and my other friend Rachel and that's just the ones I know about. So I really can't understand why I'm so pissed off with you!

TISH: I'm sorry.

KATE: Except, of course, you've both been lying to me and laughing at me all day!

TISH: I haven't . . .

KATE: And letting me think that just for once things might be different. Just once I might not be being dumped on.

(NICK *appears briefly, unseen by* TISH *or* KATE. *He hears the row and disappears again.*)

Just once I might have met a woman with more interest in me than in him. Just one woman who didn't regard me with complete bloody contempt!

TISH: (*With difficulty*) I like you.

KATE: Well, I hate your fucking guts. I hate your face and your hair, I hate your sexy little body and your stupid little voice and every last ounce of cuteness in you!

(TISH *now has trouble breathing.*)

And I hate your bloody hay fever and your coughing and sneezing and the rash on your neck you think you're hiding! And if this is what they call an asthma attack then I have to say that it's pathetically predictable.

(TISH *tries to speak but cannot.*)

I hope it was nothing casual! I hope you love him! I hope you love him more than you've loved anyone because then I can watch him break your fucking heart!

(TISH *collapses, sits on the floor.*)

Stop it. Stop it!

(*She throws a glass of stale beer into* TISH's *face.*)

TISH: You're just jealous! I'm pretty. I can't help it, I like it. I'm a pretty girl.

KATE: You're a piece of arse. You're meat. It's you that brings the butchers out to play, not me!

(*A stranger enters. He fits the description we heard earlier.*)

My, look. A tall, gaunt man, middle fifties. Help yourself.
(KATE *leaves*.)

(*The following scene between* TISH *and the* MAN *is accompanied by an off-stage argument between* KATE *and* NICK. *The argument is not completely audible*.)

(TISH's *body goes rigid when she recognizes the* MAN. *She seems terrified. She has difficulty getting to her feet, but when the* MAN *takes a step towards her she stumbles backwards, knocks over a chair, and ends up on the floor again*.)

MAN: Hello, sweetheart.

TISH: Leave me alone!

(*The* MAN *crosses to her and kneels down beside her. He helps her sit up so that she can breath more easily. He looks around and finds her asthma spray. The* MAN *gives* TISH *the spray*. TISH *throws it aside. The* MAN *retrieves it and discovers that it's empty. He finds her bag and looks in it for another, but finds nothing. He stands and looks for the window in order to open it for some fresh air, but all the windows are boarded up. He helps her stand*.)

TISH: Leave me alone.

MAN: Upsadaisy.

TISH: I don't want to upsadaisy.

MAN: You're coming with me.

KATE: Nick!

NICK: Ho Ho Ho!

KATE: You sod.

NICK: What?

KATE: I said you sod.

NICK: How charming.

KATE: Lying, scheming sod.

NICK: Kate . . .

KATE: Don't 'Kate' me!

NICK: Listen . . .

KATE: I've had it with you.

NICK: Calm down.

KATE: Fuck off!

NICK: Just calm down.

KATE: Don't you tell me to calm down!

NICK: Well, don't fucking calm down then, I don't care.

KATE: I think you're a pig. I think you're a complete pig.

NICK: Why?

KATE: You know why!

NICK: I don't.

KATE: You promised me!

NICK: Oh fuck.

KATE: That's right. Oh fuck.

NICK: Kate . . .

KATE: Kate's found out. Oh fuck.

NICK: Look, who left who?

KATE: And I've been back two

TISH: No!

MAN: Come on.

TISH: But I'm happy here.

MAN: Come on.

TISH: I'm happy here.

MAN: Shh. Be a good girl.
(*The* MAN *is leading her out.*)

TISH: I've got friends here.

MAN: Shhh. You need some air.

TISH: Umm . . .

MAN: Come on, sweetheart.
(*The* MAN *leads her off.*)

hours. And you've lied your fucking head off already.

NICK: Kate, this is real life, not *Dallas*. Do you think you could keep your voice down?

KATE: Don't you tell me what to . . .

NICK: Calm down.

KATE: No, I won't fucking calm down!

NICK: Look . . .

KATE: Don't touch me! Don't touch me! And don't bloody walk away from me either!

NICK: Sorry.

KATE: You don't know the meaning of the word.

NICK: I thought we'd made an agreement.

KATE: Oh yes, our agreement.

NICK: Yes, our agreement.

KATE: Your agreement.

NICK: Our agreement.

KATE: Bollocks to our agreement.

NICK: Oh, fine. Kate doesn't like it, bollocks to it. I wish you'd fucking grow up.

KATE: What did you say?

NICK: I said grow up.

KATE: Me grow up?

NICK: Yes, you grow up.

KATE: You're telling me to grow up.

NICK: You're acting like . . .

KATE: You're the one who should bloody well grow up! You're the one still chasing girls round the playground!

NICK: You're acting like a twelve year old.

KATE: Come here. Bloody well come here when I'm talking to you!

(*The argument continues until* TISH *and the* MAN *have gone. Then* NICK *evidently walks away from* KATE *and back into the room where he savagely lays into the cardboard cut-out.* KATE *follows him in.*)

KATE: If you want me to act like an adult, then start acting like one yourself!

NICK: Actually, calling you a child is unfair to children. I'd say your problem is you're stuck in adolescence. Just don't bloody tell me to grow up, all right!

(KATE *has noticed* TISH*'s absence.*)

KATE: Where's Tish?

NICK: Grow up yourself.

KATE: Where's Tish? Nick, where is she?

(KATE *checks the back room.* KEITH *enters from the main doors with a microphone which he puts into the stand.* KATE *returns and rushes out of the main doors. We hear her run down a few stairs.*)

(*Off*) Tish!

(KATE *returns.*)

Have you seen Tish? Keith, have you seen her?

KEITH: Er, yeah. She was downstairs with some bloke.

(KATE *turns again.*)

I don't think you'll catch her. They were getting into a BMW. Tasty motor.

(KATE *sits quietly, very worried.*)

NICK: It'll probably be a full house tonight. We've had a block booking from EXIT. I hope you decide to be funny.

(*Lights fade. Sound of audience chattering. Lights up. It is a*

52

few hours later and KATE *stands in a spotlight in the middle of her routine. She is initially drunk and punchy, full of a nervous sort of confidence, making much of it up.*)

KATE: . . . who the fuck wants to be Diane Keaton anyway? I mean every man you meet; every man you meet nowadays thinks he's Woody Allen. At least they all used to try to be Paul Newman or De Niro or someone; now you're expected to wet your pants for the Dudley Moore look. But Woody Allen's the one with a lot to answer for. He invented sensitive chic for men. Nowadays if a bloke ejaculates prematurely you have to respect him for it! Coming before your zip's undone is the sensitive thing to do, right? 'I'm sorry, you're just so beautiful, I'm going to come. I just have to come . . .' Bollocks to that. OK, so you can't stop them but you can tell them, 'Specs off, Woody, get that witty little tongue down there.'

MALE HECKLER: Balls.

KATE: New balls. Match point. You know, it used to worry me that there was no female equivalent for balls. I was thinking about it earlier. A bloke has got a lot of balls, right? So what does a good woman have a lot of? She can't have a lot of tit, because that's male territory; they stole that word already. Have you noticed how they hate us to use that word? You only have to mention your tits and it's:

'Don't say that.'

'What?'

'Don't call them that.'

'Don't call what what?'

'Your tits, don't call your tits er, that.'

'Darling, you are really getting on my bazooms.'

Anyway, they also stole the word cunt. A man's got balls and that's good, but it's tricky for a woman to have cunt. She can be one, as most men will tell you, but she can't have one. She has to have a vagina. It used to worry me but I finally worked it out. What women have got a lot of, if men have got a lot of balls, what we've got a lot of is, we've got a lot of clit. Clit. Anyone find clit unacceptable? You need a lot of clit to stand up and say clit in a place like this, you know? Could that be because no man ever said it? Well, one thing's for sure, there are men who are the biggest breasts you could meet, and there are some who are right vaginas, but no man ever had an ounce of clit in him. Clit power!

All right, I want hands up all the women here tonight who, in the middle of a conversation about Kierkegaard or Mahatma Gandhi or bloody Buñuel, have come on? I don't know about you but I only ever come on in cinemas, tube trains, and the flats of total strangers. And it's never the right-on strangers who keep the Tampax on the back of the loo; it's the ones who have spotless bathrooms with cheese-plants. While you're looking for the Tampax you find out how they keep it so spotless. You open the bathroom cabinet and Boots' warehouse falls into the bath. But the worst time . . . have you ever tried finding a box of Tampax at 8.30 on a Saturday night in an Indian supermarket? You never know if they'll be under the Domestos or next to the Alpen. At least in Sainsbury's they're always in the same place. Hidden behind the sugar. Oh, the curse. (*She takes a drink*.) Have you ever had a bloke undress you and he's got this fantastic tongue? It's been down your throat and in your ear and you've gotten over the initial nausea and think you could be on to a good thing . . . But you feel you ought to tell him so you say, 'I think I ought to tell you; I've got my period.' Then you ask a really silly question. You say, 'Do you mind?' It's a stupid question because the answer is always the same: 'Of course I don't mind. Of course I don't. Christ, is it one o'clock already? Look, I have to sign on in the morning . . .' Blood without violence; nice, warm harmless bleeding. Freaks 'em.

In fact a lot of things to do with sex freak men out, have you noticed? However hip they may be. You know the type who think contraception is sexy?

'You want to put my rubber on for me, baby?'

'Sure. You want to put my cap in for me?'

No way. Banished to the bathroom.

Men are definitely squeamish about any aspect of sex that doesn't go bumpity bumpity. At bumpity bumpity they're great for short and concentrated periods of time, but most exploration is definitely out. Personally, I measure a man's sensitivity and his degree of sensual and spiritual enlightenment by how much he'll let you fool around with his arsehole.

'Hey, what are you doing? I'm not into that. Not me, honey.'

It just doesn't work both ways, men do not like to be fooled around with. They don't like their willies waggled. They like their willies to be treated with reverence or at least with the same amount of respect as you treat the AA man. If he salutes.

I don't know, that's their problem. My problem, and here we get to the nitty gritty as far as I can see it, my problem is however right on I get, however much feminism I absorb and believe in and act on, and I do, I am a feminist, but I'm also a heterosexual; so however strong I get there's still a part of me that just wants to be fucked. It just wants to lie there and get screwed around with. I mean even if you take the initiative, somehow you still end up being the fuckee and not the fucker.

(*A* HECKLER *blows a raspberry.*)

Oh, well done. Can you make that noise with your mouth as well? You're a very clever boy, aren't you? Did your mother bring you? Oh no, he's with his girlfriend. Is he always so erudite, love?

HECKLER: I think your material's sexist and an insult to the entire women's movement.

KATE: (*To* GIRLFRIEND) What do you do, fuck him for practice?

HECKLER: It's inverted pornography.

KATE: Oh shut up. Just fucking shut up . . . umm . . .

(*She loses her place and some of her poise. A strange pause.*)

I know. I know. Has any man ever dragged you to one of those dreadful killer thrillers? You know, Saturday the Fourteenth Part Thirteen, free pair of 3D glasses and a meat skewer on your way in. The left-hand side of the auditorium has been reserved for those members of the audience who would prefer not to go up in smoke. It's always the same; some seven-foot retard stabbing and shooting and drilling his way through the Class of '83,

Normal Town High, Mid-America. Where the guys spend all their time talking about the girls and the girls spend all their time taking showers. It's the Black and Decker School of Suspense. And these dumb women and their dumb kid sisters have pyjama parties and watch Frankenstein on TV while one by one they're decapitated in Daddy's convertible or roasted in the microwave. And the thing is it has to be a surprise who's doing it. It's got to be the little bloke with glasses or his mother, or it's got to be the heroine's boyfriend . . . someone this last surviving, blood-spattered, half-naked woman is going to run to for help in the final minutes and almost get her throat cut and she'll have to resort to a slow-motion knitting needle through the brain or chop his head off. That last bit's the only bit I enjoy. I have this fantasy, I want to make one. I want to make a killer thriller where they've got the bloke who's been doing it, they've snapped his drill off, there's blood all over the place and they slowly pull off his rubber mask . . . and find a complete and utter stranger. A no one. Never seen him before. End of film. Wouldn't that make a crappy thriller? (*Pause.*) But that's how it happens. It's always some stranger. . . (*Pause.*) Some bloke . . . (*Pause.*) Ummm . . . Sorry.

(*She loses it.*)

HECKLER: Boring!

KATE: Boring. Right. Umm . . .

(*Pause. She is not with it now. If* NICK *or* KEITH *is visible they show slight concern.*)

That's right, there's only one sin, isn't there? Thou shalt not be boring. You can be racist, sexist, downright bad, but if you're boring it's not show business. I'll tell you why you're bored. You're bored because I'm a woman, you can't see my tits, and nobody's about to dismember me. I only talk about it, right? Jesus, he's right. I give it to you verbally. That's what he meant, right? All right, I admit it. Guilty. I'm guilty. OK. So, no more rude words. I promise. No more porn. So, what now?

(*Pause.*)

HECKLER: Boring!

KATE: So now I'm boring! Whoops. Oh fuck, I'm boring. And guilty. And you paid to get in. That's the next point you're going to bring up, right? Your petty fucking admission. All right, what do you want? What do you want? You want the strip? Tits and arse? Hard fucking cheese.

(KATE *is very disturbed. She clambers off the stage and through the barhatch.*)

OK. Right. This is what you get in the movies. Did you know ketchup used to have tomatoes in it? That's where it got its name. This is what you get in the movies.

(*She picks up one of the knives behind the bar and pretends to cut her throat with it while squirting ketchup all over the place.*)

And that's just the first murder. You get disembowellings and chainsaws later. Don't go away.

(*She disappears for a moment and returns with a large cleaver. She returns to the stage.* NICK *appears at a side door to see what's going on.*)

OK. No more boredom. Promise. I'll do the butcher routine for you. There was a German artist resorted to this. Listen. Listen to me! People didn't like this German artist's performance pieces. They didn't 'get' them. So he thought up something more direct; something they'd be sure to get. He began to cut off his toes. Then when no one got that he began to cut off his fingers. That was his gig. He'd do some stuff, then cut off another finger. And still no one knew what the fuck he was on about. So finally in a small cellar club in Berlin in 1951 he surgically removed his own arm. Sold out that gig. And everyone had stopped giving a shit what it meant anyway. Off came the arm. Then he died, which was a shame because he'd been offered a season. Just him and an industrial mincer. But it's true, the rest of it. That's what the people wanted. They were bored. He did his best.

So . . . what I want is a show of hands . . . I need a good majority, but if I get it I'll give you a finger. Or if it's unanimous a whole hand. No, perhaps not a whole hand. But a finger. Hands up for a finger. My finger, promise.

(*Pause.*)

No takers. House full of humanitarians is what we have

here. Or could it be a houseful of sick, voyeuristic trendies who are too shy to put up their pandies? OK, let's turn it around. I want a majority of hands in the air or you get a finger whether you like it or not.

(*Pause.*)

Come on. A couple of hands. Anyone?

(*Pause.*)

OK. In all seriousness. Deadly seriousness. I've got a finger at stake here. If the majority of you will not put your hands in the air I shall cut my pinky off. I never use it anyway. It has no function. Come on, I want hands. I'm serious. I mean it. No joke. Hands up unless you want me to maim myself for you. You've got thirty seconds.

(*Pause. A long one.* KATE *picks up the cleaver and waggles her little finger.* HARRY's *hand goes up.* NICK's *hand goes up.* KEITH's *hand is already up.*)

Thank you. That's nice of you. Four, no five hands out of what? A hundred and fifty? Thank you. Five kind hands. Not enough.

(*She brings the cleaver down on her finger. There is general consternation.*)

Is anyone still bored?

(NICK *jumps onstage but she swings the cleaver lazily to keep him away.*)

Careful. I'm probably famous now. All I need is a pianist. And er . . . wow. Pain is always such a fucking surprise, isn't it? Every time. Well, I reckon I've got a good nine gigs left and then there's a problem. Tuesday week I shall have run out of bookings and won't be able to sign my dole card. Ow! Jesus.

(*She collapses.* NICK *runs to her and is generally useless.* HARRY *is the one who picks her up.*)

HARRY: (*To* NICK) Get rid of them.

(NICK *looks blankly at* HARRY.)

Clear the bloody room.

KEITH: Does it hurt?

KATE: Only when I laugh.

(KATE *passes out.* HARRY *picks her up . . . The lights fade.*

When the lights come up again ten minutes have passed. The
room is empty but for KATE, HARRY *and* KEITH. HARRY *has*
almost completed bandaging KATE'*s hand.* KEITH *is showing*
her a trick. He completes it.)

KATE: Do it again.
(*Does it.*)
Do it again.
(*Does it.*)
Do it again.
(*Does it.*)
Ow!

HARRY: Sorry.

KATE: How's it done?

KEITH: Ahah.

KATE: Fuckwit.

KEITH: I don't know why it irritates people so much that I
won't tell them. I've had whole relationships go west
because I wouldn't tell them how some stupid trick's done.

KATE: Because it's bloody infuriating.

KEITH: But if I do tell, they're so unimpressed they tend to lose
interest anyway.
(KEITH *sits in the corner.*)

HARRY: How's that?

KATE: Thank you.
(NICK *enters, white as a sheet.*)

NICK: They're on their way. It's fucking bedlam down there.

HARRY: OK. Sit with her.
(*Exit* HARRY.)

NICK: I don't know what to say really. I'm irresponsible. I lied
to you. I lie to you. A lot. I don't take you seriously. Or
Pattie. And I fuck around. I admit it. I fuck around. But
you shouldn't have done that.

KATE: What?

NICK: The thing is . . . I really like making love to women.
Different women. I mean there are so many of you. I mean,
remember the first time? It's always best that first time. Isn't it?

KATE: No.

NICK: Well, for us, for me. Look, what I'm trying to say . . .

Whatever I do, whatever I am, it is you, Kate. So you didn't have to do that.

KATE: This may come as a hell of a shock, but I didn't do it because of you.

NICK: Mmmm? Sure.

KATE: As a matter of fact, I meant to miss.

(NICK *looks at her in disbelief, then laughs*.)

Ha ha.

(*He kisses her*.)

And who was that?

NICK: No one.

KATE: That doesn't mean it was you, Nick, that means it was no one. No, don't touch me. I don't think I want you to touch me ever again, thank you. In fact, if you so much as lay a finger on me . . . (*She smiles*.) I'll remove it.

(*They stare at each other. Enter* HARRY.)

HARRY: There's a vanload of black fellers just arrived. They want to talk to you.

NICK: Shit.

HARRY: And it's gone last orders.

(*Exit* NICK. HARRY *looks out of the window*.)

KATE: Keith?

KEITH: Yeah?

KATE: Show me that trick again.

(*He does*.)

And again.

(*He does*.)

And again.

(*He does*.)

Yeah, I saw it that time.

HARRY: I think he's going to have some trouble with that big one. I think he could do with some moral support.

KEITH: Right. Um. Right.

(*Exit* KEITH.)

KATE: Thank you, Harry.

HARRY: I think you should take some advice. I think you should take a good look at yourself and tell yourself quite honestly what it is you don't like about yourself. And you

know what it'll be? If you're truly honest you'll find the
thing you don't like about yourself is your dreadful haircut.
Take my advice and grow your hair. Long. Like it was
when you were a girl. You'll feel a new woman.
(KATE *smiles tightly and makes a rude gesture.* HARRY *looks
down out of the window.*)
It's snowing again.
(*An ambulance siren is heard in the distance.*)
HARRY: Two minutes, princess, then you'll be on your way.
(HARRY *leaves.* KATE *surveys the damage to her hand, takes a
drink of the brandy beside her. The* MAN *enters. She freezes.*)
MAN: Are you Kate?
KATE: Where's Tish?
MAN: She asked me to come. We left some of her things.
KATE: Who are you?
MAN: I'm her father. Are you all right?
KATE: Where is she?
MAN: The Kensington. She's had a rather bad attack. You must
have realized how ill she is; it astonishes me none of you did
anything for her.
KATE: Well, what's wrong with her?
MAN: One doctor put it quite succinctly. He said for some girls
there comes a time when the body turns against the mind
and says, 'Enough. I want to stop this now.' Evidently it's
becoming quite common in one form or another. Patricia
said you were a friend of hers. She asked me to give you
this.
(*He hands* KATE *a note.*)
I've been looking for her since the end of summer. I'm
taking her home, or at least somewhere she can breathe.
Thank you for taking such good care of her.
(*He takes* TISH's *things and leaves.* KATE *reads the note.*
HARRY *returns.*)
HARRY: Any minute now.
KATE: You know the trouble with me, Harry? I get so angry I
don't know who I hate.
HARRY: The roads'll be bad.
(*The lights fade.*)

61

EPILOGUE

A cottage on Dartmoor. The furnishings are very sparse and are all made of wood, stone, or natural wool and cottons. TISH *is there, dressed simply in white and looking very well. The wind can be heard. The sound of a door knocking.* TISH *runs out expectantly.*

TISH: (*Off*) Wait.
    (*She runs in again, and off another way.*)
    (*Off*) Come in.
    (KATE *comes in, well dressed against the weather.*)
    (*Off*) What are you wearing?
KATE: What? Oh, um . . . (*She takes off her parka.*) I don't know.
TISH: (*Off*) It's only wool or cotton, I'm afraid. Anything nylon or acrylic or anything . . .
KATE: Shit.
TISH: (*Off*) I'm sorry.
KATE: No, it's all right. I didn't think.
    (*Looking at the labels of her clothes,* KATE *finds she has to strip down to her underwear. This she does with increasing reluctance. The cottage is very cold.*)
TISH: (*Off*) I'm really sorry.
KATE: Don't apologize. Look, the rest's Marks and Spark's. One hundred per cent cotton. Promise.
    (TISH *comes in.*)
TISH: I'm sorry. Here.
    (*She offers her a blanket or sheet.*)
KATE: Hello.
TISH: Hello.
KATE: You're looking well.
TISH: I am well. That's why I'm being so careful. Daddy's spent a fortune on this place. He comes up all he can. And there's a girl in the village who rides up every other day. . .
KATE: You must be lonely as hell.
TISH: But I'm well. Breathe. Just breathe. Isn't the air wonderful?

KATE: Not all over.

TISH: Are you cold?

KATE: I don't know. I can't actually feel my body.

TISH: I'm sorry. I've gotten used to the cold.

KATE: Well, it's all right for you. You've got more clothes on than usual. I'm sorry about that awful day. Nick's gone to New York to be famous now. Keith's doing TIE in Watford. The circuit took over the pub; now it's all slagging off the left or putting fish down your trousers really.

TISH: How's your hand?

KATE: Oh, healing. It'll be OK. God, it's quiet. What do you do out here on your own?

TISH: I look out of the window. The night I arrived I couldn't sleep so I got up and tried to see out; but it was very black. Cold. All I could see was my own reflection in the glass. So I sat there and looked at myself until morning. And as the sun came up I began to fade away and beyond the glass the most fantastic landscape happened. The view is wonderful. I used to spend a lot of time looking in mirrors; preparing myself, beautifying. Then I'd do the act and they'd all agree I was very special and I'd smile and go back to the mirror. Now I spend all that time at the window, or the one in the other room. Sometimes as it gets dark I begin to see myself again . . . but there's no need to look any more. I turn on the lights and read a book. Would you like some tea?

KATE: Thanks.

(TISH *goes to the door*.)

Tish?

TISH: Yes?

KATE: Could we er . . . could we sort of cuddle up to each other for a moment? I just mean . . .

(KATE *fights back tears. With great relief*, TISH *runs to comfort her. They kiss each other*.)

TISH: Think of a colour.

KATE: What?

TISH: Close your eyes and think of a colour.

(TISH *presses her forehead tightly to* KATE's *for five or six seconds then pulls away.*)

Yellow.

KATE: That's astonishing. Do it again.

(*They repeat the procedure.*)

TISH: Pink.

KATE: I don't believe it.

TISH: It's easy. It's obvious really; that's where you think, so if you put them together and think hard enough . . . You try it. Just make your mind blank for a second, then try it.

(KATE *tries it, then, with great hesitation:*)

KATE: Blue. Blue?

(TISH *smiles.*)

TISH: Blue.

KATE: Sky blue or sea blue?

TISH: Sky blue.

(*Pause.*)

You will stay for a while, won't you?

KATE: I have to go to Brighton. Come with me.

SLOW FADE